The Romper Room™
Bedtime Storybook

Library of Congress Cataloging in Publication Data

Karnovsky, B. N. S.
The Romper room bedtime story book.

Summary: Nine illustrated stories relate the adventures
of Romper Room characters Up-Up, Granny Cat, and Kimball.
1. Children's stories, American. [1. Short stories]
I. Williams, A. O., ill.   II. Title.
PZ7.K144Ro 1984   [E]   82-46039
ISBN 0-385-18310-0

Printed in Italy

THE ROMPER ROOM™ BEDTIME STORYBOOK

By B.N.S. Karnovsky

Illustrated by A. O. Williams

Doubleday & Company, Inc.   Garden City, New York

To The Parent

It is a rare parent indeed who, tucking a young one into bed, has never heard the plea "Read me a story!"

While the importance of being able to read is widely accepted in our society, what is generally less well understood is how we can help our children learn to actually *enjoy* reading. Experts agree that two sure ways to encourage your children's love of books are to let them see you, the parent, reading for recreation, and to read to them regularly. And bedtime seems to be a favorite time to read to children, for reasons shared by both parent and child.

Dinner is over, toys have been put away, and the pressures of the day are finally over. Well, almost—there still remains the problem of how to lure the rambunctious youngster up to bed. The prospect of a bedtime story and your reassuring presence, however, can transform this "curfew" into an occasion for fantasy and delight. A quiet story just before the lights go off can also soothe the child and help him or her drift gently off to sleep.

Reading a bedtime story is one of the best ways to show that you care. It's a loving and private time for just the two of you, an opportunity to build a lasting rapport between you and your child.

Professor Gilbert Schiffman, Ed.D.
Professor Paul R. Daniels, Ed.D.

Department of Education, Johns Hopkins University

Contents

FAIRY TALES

One day UpUp found himself walking on a narrow path in a deep, dark forest. He had never been there before and he had no idea how he'd gotten there. He wasn't even sure where he was headed. UpUp was *very* confused.

Suddenly he saw three small pigs coming toward him on the path. The first pig carried a pile of straw. The second one had a bundle of sticks tied to his back, and the third pig was struggling with a load of bricks.

"Hmm," UpUp said to himself as the three pigs went by him. "These pigs look *very* familiar."

9

No sooner had the three pigs passed than a large egg rolled by. This was no ordinary egg, though. It had a big smile on its face and a golden crown on its head. It was Humpty Dumpty!

"Hey, Humpty!" UpUp shouted. "Where are you going?"

"I'm meeting some very important people at the town wall," Humpty Dumpty answered.

And with that, he rolled down the path. UpUp was still staring after him when he heard footsteps behind him. He turned and saw a beautiful princess who was obviously in a great hurry. She was followed closely by seven peculiar little men with beards.

"Excuse me," she said to UpUp, "but I'm looking for an old woman selling bright red apples. Have you seen her?"

This was too much for UpUp.

"Just a minute," he said. "Isn't your name Snow White?"

"Yes," she replied, "and please let me pass. I must find one of those apples!"

She ran past him and the seven dwarfs bumped and pushed UpUp aside to keep up with her. As soon as they had all gone by, a little girl appeared. She wore a long red cape and carried a big basket.

"Let me guess," UpUp said to her. "I suppose you're on your way to your grandmother's house?"

"Why, that's right," said the little girl. "She's not at all well, and I've got a basket of goodies for her."

UpUp couldn't stand it anymore. He ran as fast as he could passing Snow White, the seven dwarfs, Humpty Dumpty, and, finally, the Three Little Pigs. When he got to the front of the line, UpUp stood there and blocked the path.

"Wait a minute!" he shouted. "Wait a minute, please!"

Everyone stopped.

"I hate to tell you this, but you're all headed for big trouble!" UpUp said.

"Trouble?" asked Snow White. "How could that be?"

"Well," UpUp replied, "you, for instance, should *not* eat that apple. And you, Humpty, you'd better stay off that wall!"

"Don't be ridiculous," Humpty Dumpty harrumphed. "There are a *lot* of people expecting me at that wall!"

"Who, for instance?" asked UpUp.

"All the king's horses and all the king's men! That's who!" Humpty Dumpty replied.

Meanwhile, the line was getting longer and longer. Cinderella had just arrived in her carriage, and the dwarfs were tripping over Rapunzel's long hair.

"You must listen to me," said UpUp. "I'm just trying to help you! Little pigs, don't bother building the houses out of sticks and straw, because they won't last!"

"How dare you!" the Three Little Pigs exclaimed.

"Little Red Riding Hood! You should turn back now and forget about seeing Granny! Humpty! Do you want to wind up scrambled?! As for you, Cinderella, keep a close eye on the clock and don't stay out past midnight!"

UpUp could see by their angry faces that no one believed him. More important, all of them were getting more and more restless to get on with their journeys.

"We've got things to do and people to see," one of the dwarfs complained, "so get out of the road!" And with that, he pushed past UpUp.

Once the dwarfs had led the way, everyone made a mad dash to get through. UpUp tried to stay where he was, but they were all bumping and pushing and shoving him around. Cinderella's carriage was headed straight toward him when he felt another shove and heard a familiar voice.

"UpUp, are you listening?" It was Granny! UpUp was home in his favorite chair.

"Huh?" UpUp said, opening his eyes.

"You fell asleep, UpUp," Granny said, "and I must say, I think it's rather rude. If you want me to read you a fairy tale, you've got to stay awake."

"I'll stay awake, I promise!" UpUp said. He meant it, too.

"Very well, then." Granny continued, "Once upon a time, there were three bears..."

UpUp smiled. Three *bears,* he thought. *It's a good thing I didn't run into them!*

THE LOST RING

"Oh dear, Kimble, I've lost it!" Granny said. She was terribly upset.

"Lost what?" Kimble asked.

"The ring!"

"Oh no, not the ring!" Kimble exclaimed. "What ring?"

"My Great-Aunt Kitty's ring. The ring that belonged to the queen of the Kitty Cat Kingdom."

"Your great Aunt Kitty was queen of the Kitty Cat Kingdom?"

"Well," Granny explained, "the fact is, long, long ago, the old queen had died, and a new queen had not yet been named. My Great-Aunt Kitty had been given the ring to hold until all the cats could agree on a queen. Well, as you know, getting cats to agree on anything can take quite a while, so finally Aunt Kitty was asked to take the ring to Italy for safe keeping."

"No!" Kimble said. "To Italy! Where is Italy?"

"Across the Atlantic Ocean and very far away, dear," Granny continued. "So she set sail with the ring safely tucked away, and everything was going well until a pirate ship stopped her boat in the middle of the ocean."

"A pirate ship! With pirates?" Kimble was getting very excited.

"Yes," Granny said. "And the pirate king's name was the Great Kimbali."

Kimble was terribly excited now. He imagined two great ships at sea, with a beautiful Aunt Kitty and a tall, mustachioed pirate named Kimbali.

"As I was saying," Granny went on, "my Great-Aunt Kitty had this very valuable ring with her. She didn't want the pirates to get it, so she hid it in her cabin.

"'Give me all your jewels,' the pirate Kimbali commanded, 'or I will make you walk the plank!'

"All the passengers on board gave Kimbali their jewels, but Aunt Kitty had already hidden the ring, so the pirates didn't get it."

"'The Kitty Cat Kingdom ring,' Kimbali shouted, 'is not here! I know one of you has it!'"

"When Aunt Kitty heard that, she ran down to her cabin with the fierce pirate Kimbali chasing after her. Aunt Kitty was scared down to her tail, but she knew it was her duty to protect the ring."

By now Kimble was completely caught up in the story. He stomped through Granny's house as he imagined Kimbali the Pirate had stomped through the ship. Granny went on with the story.

"'Give me the ring!' the Great Kimbali shouted."

"'Never, never...' cried Aunt Kitty."

"'I'll find it myself then!' the Great Kimbali roared. And with that, he went to her chest of drawers and pulled out the ring."

Granny watched as Kimble stomped past her. He opened the nearest drawer and took out a velvet box. He opened the lid, and gasped. It was the lost ring!

"Kimble, you found the ring, just like the Great Kimbali did!"

"I found the ring! I found the ring!" Kimble was thrilled. "Ooh, what did your Great-Aunt Kitty do when *Kimbali* found the ring?"

"Aunt Kitty snatched the ring away from Kimbali, placed it over her heart and said, 'Kimbali, to get this ring, you will have to run your pirate sword through my heart!'"

"No!" Kimble said. "How brave! How true! What happened then?"

"Well, Kimble," Granny said, "pirates live by certain rules, and one of them is that they will not kill any lady pure of heart. When Kimbali saw that Aunt Kitty meant exactly what she said, he put his sword away, bowed, and let Aunt Kitty keep the ring."

"Like this?" Kimble asked as he bowed deeply.

"Yes, I'm sure it happened *just* that way."

"Oh, what a wonderful story!" Kimble sighed. "Then what happened?"

"The Great Kimbali stomped off the ship, never to be seen again."

"Oh, I see..." Kimble thought for a moment. "Well, the Great Kimbali might have disappeared, but I will not stomp off. I will stay with you and be your friend always."

"Thank you, Kimble. You *are* a good friend."

With that, Granny held the ring above her heart, just as her Great-Aunt Kitty might have done. She winked at Kimble and Kimble bowed. The Kitty Cat Kingdom ring was safe once more.

UPUP'S UP A TREE

One afternoon not very long ago, if you had stopped at a certain tree and looked up, you would have seen something very green in the leaves. If you had looked a little closer, you would have seen that the green thing was not a leaf—it was UpUp. How, you might wonder, did UpUp find himself in a tree, turning green?

Earlier that day, UpUp had decided he wanted a tree house. So he gathered together hammers, nails, boards, and all the rope he could find, then he lifted everything up into the tree with pulleys, climbed up the branches, and built a tree house.

UpUp had done everything right, but he forgot two things: he forgot to build a ladder, and he forgot that he was terrified of heights. As he put his tools away and sat down to admire the view, his stomach started to feel funny, and his head began to spin.

"Well, you've done it this time, mastermind," UpUp thought to himself. "I'll have to spend the rest of my life up here."

UpUp was miserable.

He was so caught up in his own problem, he didn't even notice that Kimble was standing just underneath him, looking up.

"Oh," Kimble said, "what a bee-you-ti-ful tree house! So this is where you have been, UpUp. I have been looking all over for you, and here you are, in a brand-new tree house!"

"Yes, I—ulp!—built it myself," UpUp said, trying to sound proud—and trying to look less green. For once, UpUp was not talking much. His stomach was still doing flip-flops.

"Oh, UpUp, you are a genius!" Kimble said, thrilled with his friend's work.

"Yes, I just said that to myself a minute ago." Suddenly UpUp got an idea: If he could get Kimble to come up, maybe Kimbel could help him get down.

"Say, Kimble, old buddy, how would you like to come up and see the house?"

"Really?" said Kimble. And in an instant he climbed the branches of the tree and stood next to UpUp in the tree house.

Kimble walked from one end of the tree house to the other, inspecting it closely and admiring his friend's work. "UpUp!" Kimble exclaimed. "This is a wonderful tree house! So well made, and *so* sturdy!" Kimble jumped up and down to show UpUp just how sturdy it was.

UpUp felt sicker. He was sinking fast. Kimble looked at UpUp and saw that his face was green and getting greener every second.

Kimble suddenly realized that his friend was unhappy being so high up. Kimble also understood that UpUp was too proud and too stubborn to admit he was scared.

"Say, UpUp," Kimble said softly, "I suppose you must be tired from all the work you have done today."

"What? Oh, yeah, a little, I guess."

"Well," Kimble said, "why don't you climb on my back and I'll get us down."

"Great!" UpUp shouted in delight. Then he got quiet. He didn't want Kimble to know he was scared. "Uh—I mean, that would be OK. I am a little pooped."

So UpUp got on Kimble's back, and together the two of them climbed down the branches of the tree. When they were safely down from the tree, UpUp kissed the ground. Kimble watched him.

"You and the ground are very good friends!"

"Yes," UpUp laughed. "The ground always lets you know where you stand. Do you know what I mean, old buddy?"

"Yes, and I am glad I could help you get down."

"Well," UpUp said, "so am I. But you know I could have gotten down from there myself if I hadn't been so tired."

"Of course!" Kimble agreed.

"I didn't *really* need any help."

"Oh, I know." Kimble smiled.

"I mean, it wasn't that I was scared of being too high up or anything like that."

"I understand, UpUp," Kimble said.

Then UpUp said, "But now that I've built a tree house and conquered the heights, I think it's time to move on to some new challenge." *Like building a sand castle,* he thought to himself, *or a cave, or anything close to the ground!*

THE POPCORN MACHINE

The big package UpUp had been waiting for finally arrived. He couldn't wait to open it and show Granny his newest possession—a fancy, fangle-dangled, super-duper, shiny-bright popcorn machine.

"My goodness," Granny exclaimed. "How beautiful! I've never seen so many buttons and knobs on one machine before."

UpUp smiled. "That's because it does just about everything. Press this button and it turns into a jukebox so you can pop your popcorn in time to your favorite song. Press this other button, and you can make popcorn in different colors. And if you turn this knob, you'll have popcorn balls and popcorn squares and popcorn in any shape you want!"

Granny was very much surprised, but she was even more surprised when she noticed that UpUp was about to throw out the popcorn machine's instruction book.

"Don't you think you'll need that?" she asked him.

"Who, me? Nope!" he replied as he plugged in the machine. "An expert popcorn popper like me can figure this machine out without any help." And with that, he threw the book into the trash can. Then, with a wild look in his eye, UpUp poured pounds of unpopped popcorn into the popcorn machine and turned it on.

Hmm, Granny thought, but she didn't say what she was thinking. She just picked up the instruction booklet, congratulated UpUp on his wonderful new machine, said goodbye, and walked out the door.

UpUp didn't even notice her leave. He was too busy pressing buttons and turning knobs. Within seconds, golden kernels of popcorn began jumping up and down.

"I'm rich!" UpUp screamed in delight. "Popcorn! Popcorn for days, weeks, months, years!" Then UpUp went to his cupboards and poured all of his popcorn into the machine.

26

Slowly at first, the machine began turning out popcorn. It filled a bag, then two, then three. As it cooked more popcorn, UpUp started to have trouble keeping up. He would run to the kitchen, grab a bag, run back to the machine, fill the bag, then run back to the kitchen for another one. Soon after he'd filled all his bags, he realized that he had enough popcorn. He pressed what he thought was the STOP button. But the machine didn't stop. Instead, it began to play disco music. Now the popcorn started popping faster, popping in time to the music. UpUp pressed another button. He was sure this one would stop the machine. But it didn't. Instead, lights started flashing and blinking on and off, and the music became louder and louder.

Now UpUp could hardly keep up with the popcorn. He filled his kitchen drawers, the kitchen sink, the bathtub. Finally, even his closets were overflowing with popcorn.

UpUp wanted the machine to stop! He turned a knob. Suddenly popcorn started popping out red, orange, blue, yellow, green, pink, purple—all different colors. UpUp couldn't stop it. His living room was two feet deep in popcorn. He pressed more buttons. He turned more knobs. Still, the machine didn't stop. It began popping out popcorn balls, popcorn squares, popcorn triangles. There was popcorn everywhere!

"Oh-oh," UpUp said. "I think this might be too much of a good thing!"

He was right. Wave upon wave of popcorn flowed out of the machine. The popcorn waves swept UpUp around the living room.

"Ulp, glub—help!" UpUp yelled.

Just then, Granny and Kimble knocked on UpUp's door. UpUp screamed for them to open it.

Kimble did. He was bowled over by a flood of popcorn. Granny luckily stepped aside. As the popcorn came tumbling out, so did UpUp.

Granny saw what was happening and knew right away what to do. She got a shovel from UpUp's garage and she began to dig her way through the popcorn toward the machine, which was still popping full blast.

"There's no way to stop it!" UpUp shouted over the music.

"Oh, nonsense!" Granny shouted back at him.

By now she had cut a path through the mountain of popcorn. She reached around to the back of the machine and flipped a switch marked "OFF." Suddenly the machine stopped beeping, bopping, and popping.

"Hooray for Granny!" Kimble shouted. "You stopped the popcorn machine!"

"Gee...uh...thanks, Granny. I was just about to push that button myself," UpUp said.

Granny smiled and handed him the instruction book. Then UpUp added, "It might come in handy —even for an expert like me."

Granny hugged him and laughed and said, "Let's have some popcorn."

"Yes," Kimble chimed in. "Let's have some popcorn!"

"OK," UpUp said. "It just so happens I made enough for everyone."

And with that he dived into a mountain of popcorn and started munching happily.

TEE HEE, THE EXTRA-FUNNY EXTRATERRESTRIAL

Late one night Kimble was sitting up in bed, looking through his favorite picture book. Suddenly the lights in his room blinked on and off, the walls shook for a moment, and there was a loud noise outside.

CLUNK! It sounded as if something heavy had dropped from the sky.

Kimble opened his bedroom window. He heard a strange, high, squeaky sound—something was out there....

Kimble decided to find out what it was. He went to the back door and opened it. It was *very* dark, and he was *very* scared. Then he heard the squeaky noise again. Kimble looked and saw where the noise was coming from. He couldn't believe his eyes!

"Oh, my!" Kimble gasped.

There in his backyard, a strange little glowing man
was talking and laughing. Even stranger, though,
was the fact that the little man was talking to a small
spaceship.

"Oh!" Kimble exclaimed. "I can't believe it! You
must be from outer space!"

The little man stopped laughing.

"Yes," he said. "My name is Tee Hee."

He put out what looked a little like a glowing
hand—Kimble wasn't sure whether to shake it or
not. So he bowed instead.

"I am Kimble," Kimble said. "And I officially

welcome you to Earth and to my backyard. How long
will you be staying?"

"Forever, I'm afraid." Tee Hee sighed. His warm
glow was beginning to fade. "I seem to have run out
of fuel for my ship."

"Oh, that is easy to fix," Kimble said. "Let's go
down to the gas station and get some fuel."

"Do they have laughter there?" Tee Hee asked
with a hopeful look in his eyes.

"Laughter? No, they have gasoline."

"Then I'm afraid it's no use. You see, my ship runs
on laughter."

"Really?" Kimble said. "That is even easier. We will just tell a few jokes."

"That's the problem," Tee Hee said. "I've already used up all the jokes I know, and my ship just doesn't laugh at them anymore. Look, I'll show you: What do you get when you cross a galaxy with a toad?"

"Star warts," the ship's computer responded.

"What is an astronaut's favorite sandwich filling?"

"Launch meat," the computer answered.

"How can you tell the moon has eaten?"

"Look—up—and—see—if—it's—full."

It was just as the spaceman was telling his last joke that UpUp came by.

"I didn't know it was Halloween," UpUp said to Tee Hee. "Trick or treat?"

Tee Hee didn't understand.

UpUp walked over to Tee Hee. "Come on, take the mask off!"

"No, no! UpUp, stop," Kimble said. "This is Tee Hee. He is from outer space."

"Sure," UpUp mocked, "and I'm King Kong." UpUp didn't believe any of it until Tee Hee pointed a funny-looking stick at a garbage can, and it disappeared in a puff of smoke.

"Like I always said," UpUp went on nervously, "any outer space friend of Kimble's is a friend of mine."

That settled, Kimble told UpUp about his new friend's problem. UpUp understood—as only UpUp would.

He said, "Listen, Tee Hee old pal, I know you think this is a tough break, but take it from me, it's going to be terrific here."

Tee Hee started glowing again.

"It is?" he said.

"Sure. Look, aliens are very popular on earth right now. We can cash in on you in a very big way: TV shows, movie contracts, records, Tee Hee T-shirts. You'll be a smash!"

The ship's computer began to blink. A little smile appeared on its screen.

"A—smash?" the ship asked.

"Sure," UpUp said. "You'll make millions!"

"Millions—of—what?" the ship wanted to know.

"Dollars!" UpUp shrieked in delight.

The ship started to chuckle. The fuel gauge was moving up.

"You'll be able to buy a big Cadillac and drive it all over Hollywood," UpUp continued.

As the ship's laughter grew, Tee Hee started laughing too.

"You'll be able to buy a big house with your own private swimming pool!" UpUp was in a world of his own. "You'll even be able to buy your own video game machine!"

Finally, UpUp saw that Tee Hee was laughing so hard he could barely talk, and the ship's fuel tank was reading FULL.

"Hey," UpUp said, "wait a minute, what's so darn funny?"

Tee Hee was climbing into his ship, but he turned around and said to UpUp:

"What good is a Cadillac when I have a spaceship? And what would I do with a big house and a swimming pool in outer space?"

"But think of the money!" UpUp cried.

"Money? You can't spend Earth money in outer space. But thank you for filling up my ship's fuel tank. Goodbye. I'm going."

"Going? You can't be serious!" UpUp said.

"You're right. I am never serious," Tee Hee laughed. "I laugh my way through the stars."

And with that, the ship gave a giggle of its own and rose up into the air. Kimble waved goodbye.

UpUp screamed, "Don't go!"

But Tee Hee, the extra-funny extraterrestrial, flew off into the night.

36

WHAT DO WE DO WITH THE DRAGON?

PART I

King UpUp was in trouble. The people of his kingdom were very upset. A large, fire-breathing dragon had come to live in their kingdom.

The dragon was a big problem. When he roared, a ball of fire shot out of his mouth, burning all the farmers' crops. And when he walked through the countryside, he stomped on all the people's homes.

King UpUp knew he must do something. His reputation was at stake. After all, it was his job to take care of his kingdom and protect his people.

But time was running out. King UpUp was supposed to talk to his people from the royal balcony in just a few minutes, and he still didn't know what to do about the dragon. With nowhere else to turn, King UpUp sent for his most trusted adviser, Sir Kimble.

Sir Kimble looked through all his books and files for an answer to the problem.

Finally, holding up five pieces of paper, he said, "There are five possible answers."

"Great!" King UpUp grabbed the first answer and went out onto the balcony.

"People of my kingdom!" King UpUp began, "I have found the way to solve the problem of the terrible dragon."

The people cheered. King UpUp looked down and read aloud the writing on the paper: "WE WILL IGNORE THE DRAGON."

"What!" the villagers exclaimed. "That's impossible," somebody cried. "He's stomping on our houses!" another man shouted. "He's eating up our cows and pigs!" cried another. "And burning our fields!" The crowd started to boo. King UpUp ran back to the inner room.

"Sir Kimble, the people don't like the first answer, and I can't say that I blame them. Quick, give me another solution!"

Sir Kimble handed the king another piece of paper. King UpUp grabbed it, ran back, and read it to the crowd:

"WE CAN MOVE THE KINGDOM AWAY FROM THE DRAGON!"

Everyone was very puzzled, as this made no sense at all! They knew how hard it would be to move a castle, a kingdom, and everyone who lived there. Again, the crowd started to boo at their king.

King UpUp ran back to talk with Sir Kimble.

"Sir Kimble, the first two answers don't work. You must find a solution that will work."

"Well," Sir Kimble said, "we could try to stay out of the dragon's way. That's a third possibility."

King UpUp simply shook his head. He knew that wouldn't solve the problem.

Sir Kimble went on:

"Or, we could just give up and surrender to him. That's number four."

"No, no, that won't do at all! What's number five?" King UpUp asked.

"We can attack him!" Sir Kimble said. "We can slay the dragon, and be rid of him forever! That is answer number five."

"Attack him! Yes, that makes sense! That will make the people happy."

And, sure enough, the last answer did make the people of the kingdom happy.

"Hooray for King UpUp!" they shouted. "He is truly a good king!"

The townfolk went home feeling much relieved.

"Well, Sir Kimble, thanks a lot for your wise answer," King UpUp said. "By the way, who's going to attack the dragon?"

"I don't know," Sir Kimble said simply.

"What!" King UpUp exploded. "You're supposed to give me advice!"

Suddenly the ground shook, and a tremendous roar echoed through the castle halls.

"Oh, no!" King UpUp cried. "It's the dragon, and he's coming this way!"

They held onto each other in fear for several minutes. When nothing happened, they went to the window and saw a very peculiar sight: An old peasant woman was standing at the castle gates. Beside her, a huge dragon with pink scales snorted balls of pink smoke. From her fiery eyes, huge dragon tears fell like big white pearls. "Yoo-hoo!" cried the little peasant woman. "Please let me in! I've come a long distance from another kingdom, and I need to talk to you."

40

King UpUp went out onto the royal balcony and leaned over. The dragon started to whine loudly.

"What do you want?" King UpUp shouted.

"This is Penelope," the peasant woman said, pointing to the dragon. "And she is the answer to your problems. Let me in so I can explain."

"Another dragon is *not* the answer to my problems," King UpUp muttered. But he opened the castle gates and let them in.

PART II

King UpUp and Sir Kimble listened long into the night as the old woman explained how Penelope, the pink dragon, could save the kingdom.

"Years ago," she began, "I found Penelope lost in the woods. She was a baby, and she was so happy to see me, it didn't occur to me to be afraid of her. I took her home, and we spent many happy days together. As she grew up, she was a great help to me. In the spring she would give me some of her dragon scales to patch the leaks in the roof of my hut. In the winter she would sleep in my fireplace and keep me warm with the gentle breath of her flames."

Then the woman explained that as Penelope grew older, she became less friendly and more cranky. It was obvious that she was lonely and needed the companionship of other dragons like herself.

The peasant woman went on to say that when she heard there was a dragon in King UpUp's kingdom, she decided it would be a good idea to bring the two dragons together. "I understand dragons very well, having brought one up, and I know that a happy dragon won't cause problems. Happy dragons are peaceful and very helpful. Lonely dragons are not."

The woman spoke very convincingly. The next day, King UpUp and Sir Kimble followed behind her and Penelope as they walked toward the fierce dragon's cave.

When they arrived at the entrance, King UpUp shouted, "Hello in there! Anybody home?"

A great blast of flame and a cloud of smoke shot out from the cave entrance.

"I think he is home," Sir Kimble said in a nervous voice.

Indeed he was, and the ground shook as the dragon came out of the cave. When he saw King UpUp and Sir Kimble, he fumed and snorted. Smoke filled the air as he started toward them.

Then the dragon saw Penelope. The two of them stared at each other. For a moment, they were as still as two statues. Then, Penelope's pink scales began to shimmer in the sunlight, and the fierce dragon's gray scales began to change too. They turned a beautiful golden-orange.

King UpUp was amazed. Sir Kimble was in awe. The old woman just smiled and nodded her head.

The two dragons moved slowly toward each other.
They snorted gentle balls of perfumed smoke, and
instead of bellowing flames, they mewed and purred
softly. They drew in the claws at the end of their
paws, and reached out to each other.

"I think they like each other," the old woman said,
smiling. "And I think our problems are solved."

She was right. Everyone was happy. Penelope and the fierce dragon settled down together, and they were very peaceful and sometimes even helpful. King UpUp's kingdom was safe once again.

THE EASTER EGG HUNT

It was the morning of Dobeeville's big Easter egg hunt. A crowd had gathered in the town square. Everyone carried an empty basket, and each one hoped to fill it with the most colorful eggs and win the big first prize.

"The hunt is about to begin," the mayor of Dobeeville announced. Then he blew a loud *tweet* on a big silver whistle, and everyone was off and running— and UpUp was in the lead.

"I'm going to win that prize!" he shouted, leaving Kimble behind.

Kimble watched his friend go. "Oh well," he thought, "I guess I will have to find Easter eggs by myself."

Kimble had never been on an Easter egg hunt before, and didn't know just where to begin. He thought he spotted an egg under a nearby bush. It turned out to be nothing but a small white rock. Then he was sure he saw one in the fountain. But it was only a beam of sunlight bouncing off the water.

Where should I go? Where should I look? he wondered.

Meanwhile, UpUp was racing around ahead of the crowd. He was determined to collect the most eggs and win the prize.

Hours passed. The sun began to set. By now, everyone had returned to the town square with their baskets of eggs. Soon the winner would be announced.

UpUp counted the eggs in his basket. He was sure he had won. He looked around for Kimble, but Kimble was nowhere to be seen.

Then, UpUp spotted him. Off in the distance, Kimble was carrying something huge and round and white. He appeared to be very excited, and very tired. UpUp ran to him.

When UpUp got close enough to see what Kimble was carrying, he couldn't believe his eyes. Kimble had an egg that was bigger than any UpUp had ever seen. It was bigger than five basketballs put together.

"Kimble!" UpUp shrieked. "Where did you find that egg?"

Kimble could barely talk, he was huffing and puffing so.

"At—whew!—the museum," Kimble said.

The museum! UpUp quickly understood.

"Kimble, that's not an Easter egg! That's a dinosaur egg! You're going to get in a lot of trouble for stealing that egg!"

"Oh, dear," Kimble said.

"Kimble," UpUp went on. "Don't you know an Easter egg when you see one?"

Kimble shook his head. He was very upset. But UpUp continued.

"Just because you wanted to win the prize, that doesn't give you the right to go around taking any old egg you find."

Kimble was so upset, he nearly dropped the egg.

"Be careful!" UpUp said. He would have yelled at Kimble some more, but he was suddenly interrupted by a whole group of birds who swooped down near him.

"Are you UpUp?" the biggest bird demanded.

"Why—uh—yes, but—" UpUp looked very embarrassed.

"All right. We want out eggs back!" the birds ordered.

"Eggs?" UpUp asked innocently.

"You know, the ones you took from our nests!" said another very large bird.

Now UpUp was really embarrassed. He had wanted to win the prize so much, he, too, had gone and taken eggs that didn't belong to him.

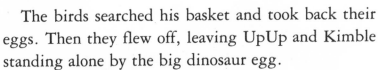

The birds searched his basket and took back their eggs. Then they flew off, leaving UpUp and Kimble standing alone by the big dinosaur egg.

"I'll help you carry this back to the museum, old buddy," UpUp said softly. He was still embarrassed. "And I'm sorry I yelled at you. . . . You can yell at me if you want to."

"No, that is all right," Kimble said.

So together they brought the egg back to the museum. Luckily no one had noticed it was missing. Outside the museum, Kimble and UpUp saw a large group of people walking home. Then they spotted Granny in the crowd: She was carrying the big chocolate rabbit. First prize!

"You won, Granny! Congratulations!" Kimble said, running up to her excitedly.

"Yeah...congratulations," UpUp chimed in, although he was a little disappointed that *he* hadn't won.

"Well, thank you, boys," Granny said. "But I'm afraid this prize leaves me with a big problem."

"A problem?" Kimble asked.

"Yes," Granny spoke, "I just know that I couldn't possibly eat all this by myself. I need some help!"

UpUp and Kimble knew just the folks who could help her, and the three friends went happily home to share the big prize.

UPUP
THE CIRCUS STAR

"The circus is coming to town!"

Kimble saw the sign posted on a fence. He ran home to tell UpUp the good news.

"Do you want to go see it with me?" he asked his friend.

"No. I'm not going to see it," UpUp replied. "I'm going to *be in* it."

Kimble's eyes opened wide. He listened as UpUp explained how he was going to get a job working under the Big Top.

"Circus folk are always looking for star quality, animal magnetism, and all-around irresistibility. And I've got plenty of all those things. They can't refuse me! I'll be a superstar!"

"Of course," Kimble agreed. "What superstar job will they give you?"

"Wait and see," was all UpUp said.

53

From that moment, UpUp wouldn't stop bragging about the job he was sure to get at the circus. He walked around as if he were the ringmaster in the center ring. He even insisted that everyone call him "the Great UpUp."

Granny found this very hard to do. It wasn't that she didn't think UpUp was great, it was just that he broke one of her dining room chairs while practicing to be a lion tamer.

"Have you ever tamed a lion?" she asked him.

"No, but I've been *your* friend for years, Granny. And you're a cat, and lions are cats. Only, they're a little bigger. It'll be a cinch."

Before she could explain the differences between herself and a lion, UpUp raised the dining room chair into the air, cracked an imaginary whip, twirled around, and—fell. That's when the chair broke. UpUp promised Granny he'd fix it.

But he never got around to it because he was too busy practicing to be a tightrope walker. That afternoon, Granny found him just as he snapped her clothesline. He'd been trying to walk across it. Luckily, he landed in a big basket of her clean laundry.

With that, he went off to Kimble's house. Kimble was eager to help him. But he didn't feel so enthusiastic after UpUp tried to juggle eggs. Instead of starting out with two or three, the way most people do when they're learning, UpUp started juggling a dozen eggs at once. Kerplop. Plop. Plop. Plop. Plop. What a mess! Broken eggs were all over the floor.

UpUp promised to wipe them up. But suddenly he looked at his watch and said, "Oh, boy. Time to go!"

"Good luck!" Kimble shouted to his friend. "Come back soon and we'll have omelets."

But UpUp didn't hear him. He was already down the road, on his way to the Big Top.

Later that evening when UpUp returned, Granny and Kimble were eager to hear the news.

"Well?" Granny asked. "What happened? Did you get a job at the circus?"

"Yes," Kimble chimed in, "what happened?"

"I got the *perfect* job. I'm the most important man in the circus! Without me the show could not go on!"

Granny and Kimble were deeply impressed.

"How wonderful!" Granny exclaimed in delight. "What do you do? Are you the lion tamer?"

"No," UpUp answered.

"The tightrope walker?"

UpUp shook his head.

"The juggler?" Kimble asked.

"No, again," UpUp said. And he refused to tell them any more except that without him there couldn't *be* a circus.

"When the crowds see me," he added, "they stand up and cheer for me. They call my name and wave their arms."

Granny and Kimble were unable to figure out what UpUp did, but they knew it had to be important.

"Well, gotta go," UpUp said. "The fans are waiting for me and I can't disappoint them." He left at once, with Granny and Kimble in total mystery. Granny spoke:

"Well, Kimble, get your hat!"

"Why?" Kimble asked. "Are we expecting rain?"

"No. We're going to the circus."

Kimble grabbed his hat and he and Granny headed toward the big tent at the edge of town.

When Kimble and Granny arrived, it was already dark. The lights made the tent look magical and exciting.

A bright spotlight lit up the center ring and the ringmaster appeared. He wore a tall black hat and he had a big mustache. It wasn't UpUp. When he blew his whistle, a band started playing and the colorful circus parade began.

Clowns ran by, doing cartwheels and throwing confetti. UpUp wasn't one of them. They were followed by a family of acrobats in sparkling blue sequined costumes. UpUp wasn't with them, either

A line of elephants marched by, holding on to each other's tails and stepping in time to the music. The circus stars riding on the elephants' backs waved and smiled at the crowd. Not one of the stars was UpUp.

Next, two cages of tigers and lions rolled by, led by the dazzling lion tamer. Behind him came the daring tightrope walker, followed by the handsome man on the flying trapeze. Then the bareback rider passed by on a beautiful white horse, followed by more horses, more clowns (who carried ducks wearing sailor hats) and dogs and daredevils. But there was still no sign of UpUp.

57

"My fur and whiskers," Granny worried. "I hope to heaven UpUp's not the one they're going to shoot out of that cannon."

But that wasn't UpUp either.

All evening long, Granny and Kimble tried to find UpUp, but they couldn't see him anywhere.

"He said the circus wouldn't be the same without him," Granny said. "Hmm, I wonder if he was fibbing?"

Just then, Granny and Kimble heard a familiar voice that rang out loud and clear.

"Popcorn! Popcorn! Get it here! Get it while it's hot! You can't watch a circus without popcorn! Get it while it's hot!"

Of course! It was UpUp! He wore a white uniform and he was selling popcorn! And the crowd *did* stand up. They waved their arms in his direction. And they called his name. "We want popcorn, UpUp!" they shouted. "We want popcorn!"

When he spotted Granny and Kimble, UpUp took a deep bow—which made him spill some popcorn. But the crowd didn't mind. They thought it was funny and they cheered and laughed. Granny and Kimble cheered and laughed too. They were glad to find their friend UpUp safe and sound, and very happy with his new job at the circus.

THE MAGIC LAMP

One day Kimble stopped by to visit his friend UpUp.

"Hello, UpUp," Kimble said.

"Hello," UpUp answered. "And goodbye. I don't have time to talk." UpUp was in the middle of a large pile of old lamps. Kimble watched for a minute. UpUp would rub each lamp, then he would look at it, and then he'd throw it aside.

"I will help you clean those lamps, UpUp. Then you will have time to talk."

Kimble picked up a lamp and started to shine it a little with his hand when a big puff of smoke came from the lamp and a huge genie appeared.

"Thank you!" said the genie in a deep voice. "At last I am free. I've been cooped up in that old lamp for years! For giving me my freedom, I will grant you three wishes."

Kimble was startled, but UpUp was jumping for joy.

"I knew there'd be a genie in one of these lamps! Yippee! Hooray! Oh boy!" UpUp shouted. Then he turned to the genie and said, "Now, genie, here's my first wish. I want—"

The genie cut him off.

"I am sorry, sir," the genie spoke, pointing to Kimble, "but *this* is the person who freed me and it is to him that I will give three wishes."

"What!" UpUp shouted. "Wait a minute, that's not fair! They're my lamps, so they're *my* wishes!"

"I'm sorry, sir, but those are the rules I've been working by for the last two thousand years," the genie said.

UpUp was furious. He turned to Kimble and screamed, "You furry flub-dub! You've done it again. I've been rubbing lamps all day long and *you* come in and ruin everything!"

Kimble was scared and a little embarrassed.

"UpUp," Kimble said, "I know you are angry, but I wish you would not yell at me."

"Your wish is my command," the genie said.

Suddenly, UpUp couldn't shout. In fact, he could barely whisper.

"Kimble," UpUp whispered, "my voice is gone."

"Oh, no!" Kimble said unhappily. "I did not mean that! I wish you had your voice back, UpUp."

"Done," replied the genie. He snapped his fingers and UpUp was once again his outspoken self.

"Kimble," UpUp said quickly, "don't say *any-thing*. Don't speak! We only have one wish left!"

"That is true." said the genie.

"Now," UpUp said, "we've got to think of a really good wish. We've only got *one* left and we can't waste it! What should we wish for? A million dollars? No, no, not enough. A ton of popcorn? No, that's too small. Hmm..." UpUp thought.

Kimble thought too.

"Oh, I wish Granny were here," Kimble finally said. "She always knows what to do."

With that, a puff of smoke filled the room and when it cleared, Granny was there.

The genie bowed.

"I have granted your three wishes and now I must return to my lamp.

"Oh, no! Don't go!" UpUp reached for the genie, but he was gone in a puff of smoke.

"My goodness!" Granny said. "Does he always come and go like that? He certainly makes a lot of smoke."

UpUp didn't hear her, though. He was too busy rubbing more lamps.